DISCARD

Sheep in a Jeep

Nancy Shaw

Sheep in a Jeep

Illustrated by Margot Apple

Houghton Mifflin Company Boston

Library of Congress Cataloging-in-Publication Data

Shaw, Nancy (Nancy E.)
  Sheep in a jeep.

  Summary: Records the misadventures of a group of
sheep that go riding in a jeep.
  [1. Stories in rhyme. 2. Sheep—Fiction]
I. Apple, Margot, Ill. II. Title.
PZ8.3.S5334Sh 1986   [E]   86-3101
ISBN 0-395-41105-X

Printed in the United States of America

RNF ISBN 0-395-41105-X
PAP ISBN 0-395-47030-7

WOZ 45 44 43 42 41 40 39

JEEP® is a registered trademark of Chrysler Corporation.

To Allison and Danny
—N.S.

To Sue Sherman
—M.A.

Beep! Beep!

Sheep in a jeep

on a hill that's

steep.

Uh-oh!

The jeep won't go.

Sheep leap

to push the jeep.

Sheep shove.

Sheep grunt.

Sheep don't think

to look up front.

Jeep goes splash!

Jeep goes thud!

Jeep goes deep

in gooey mud.

Sheep tug.

Sheep shrug.

Sheep yelp.

Sheep get help.

Jeep comes out.

Sheep shout.

Sheep cheer.

Oh, dear!

The driver sheep forgets

to steer.

Jeep in a heap.

Sheep weep.

Sheep sweep the heap.

Jeep for sale — cheap.